D0466425

NO LONGER PROPERTY OF
ANYTHINK LIBRARIES/
RANGEVIEW LIBRARY DISTRICT

Rapunzel and the Billy Goats

Crabtree Publishing Company
www.crabtreebooks.com
1-800-387-7650

PMB 59051,
350 Fifth Ave., 59th Floor
New York, NY 10118

616 Welland Ave.
St. Catharines, ON
L2M 5V6

Published by Crabtree Publishing in 2013

For Henry, Max, and Edward

Series editor: Louise John
Series Design: Emil Dacanay
Design: Lisa Peacock
Consultant: Shirley Bickler
Editor: Kathy Middleton
Proofreaders: Kelly McNiven, Crystal Sikkens
Notes to adults: Reagan Miller
Print and production coordinator: Katherine Berti

Text © Hilary Robinson 2013
Illustration © Simona Sanfilippo 2013

Printed in Canada/022013/BF20130114

All rights reserved. No part of this publication may be reproduced, stored in a retrieval system, or transmitted in any form or by any means, electronic, mechanical, photocopy, recording or otherwise, without the prior written permission of the copyright owner.

The rights of Hilary Robinson to be identified as the Author and Simona Sanfilippo to be identified as the Illustrator of this Work have been asserted.

First published in
2013 by Wayland
(A division of Hachette
Children's Books)

**Library and Archives Canada
Cataloguing in Publication**

Robinson, Hilary, 1962-
    Rapunzel and the billy goats / written by
Hilary Robinson ; illustrated by Simona Sanfilippo.

(Tadpoles: fairytale jumbles)
Issued also in electronic format.
ISBN 978-0-7787-1154-4 (bound).--ISBN 978-0-7787-
1158-2 (pbk.)

    I. Sanfilippo, Simona II. Title. III. Series:
Tadpoles (St. Catharines,
Ont.). Fairytale jumbles

PZ7.R6235Ra 2013   j823'.914   C2012-908166-3

**Library of Congress
Cataloging-in-Publication Data**

Robinson, Hilary, 1962-
 Rapunzel and the billy goats / written by Hilary
Robinson ; illustrated by Simona Sanfilippo.
       pages cm. -- (Tadpoles: fairytale jumbles)
    Summary: "Rapunzel is trapped in a high tower
by a wicked troll. The three billy goats want to help
her but the troll won't let them cross the bridge! A
handsome prince rides by on his horse. Will he be
able to help the trapped princess?"-- Provided by
publisher.
    ISBN 978-0-7787-1154-4 (reinforced library binding
: alk. paper) -- ISBN 978-0-7787-1158-2 (pbk. : alk.
paper) -- ISBN 978-1-4271-9302-5 (electronic pdf) --
ISBN 978-1-4271-9226-4 (electronic html)
    [1. Stories in rhyme. 2. Characters in literature--Fiction.] I. Sanfilippo, Simona, illustrator. II. Title.

    PZ8.3.R575Rap 2013
    [E]--dc23

                                        2012047907

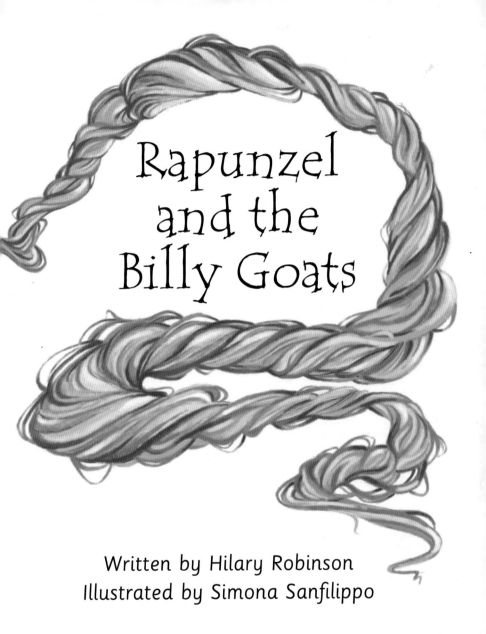

Rapunzel and the Billy Goats

Written by Hilary Robinson
Illustrated by Simona Sanfilippo

Crabtree Publishing Company
www.crabtreebooks.com

Three billy goats were grazing,
when they stopped and looked around.
They could hear a lady singing
and said, "What a lovely sound!"

They set off to a wooden bridge
by a meadow of green grass.

"Stop right there!" a mean troll yelled.
"I will not let you pass!"

7

He had built a tower by the bridge
with no door or winding stair.

And hidden at the top of it,
was Rapunzel with long, long hair.

The goats all watched the troll
as he called up to the maid,
"Rapunzel! Let down your hair!"
Then he scrambled up the braid.

One day a handsome prince rode by
and stopped to pick a flower.

He heard Rapunzel's lovely song and rode up to the tower.

Rapunzel whispered down to him,
"Please help me get out of here!"
She told him what the troll had done
and how she lived in fear.

The kindly prince said, "I'll be back with a rope to set you free!"

But the troll woke up and shouted,
"You will not escape from me!"

The troll climbed up the braid,
and he cut Rapunzel's hair!

He left her in the woods and said,
"The prince won't find you there!"

The goats took care of Rapunzel
and would come to rest by the spring.
In turn, she became a friend to them
and taught them how to sing!

The prince came back and shouted up,
"Rapunzel! Where are you?"

The troll let down Rapunzel's hair
and trapped the prince there, too.

The troll was cross and threw the prince.
Down in the bushes he lay,
blinded by thorns, until he woke
the next bright, sunny day.

He could hear the goats all singing
and Rapunzel's voice as well.

He stumbled through the leaves and trees and found them in the dell.

Rapunzel held him in her arms,
as he lay beside a tree.

Her tears of joy dripped in his eyes,
and he found that he could see!

They fell in love! As for the troll,
he was last seen heading
for far-off shores, while the billy goats
were bridesmaids at the wedding!

Notes for Adults

Tadpoles: Fairytale Jumbles are designed for transitional and early fluent readers. The books may also be used for a read-aloud or shared reading with younger children. **Tadpoles: Fairytale Jumbles** are humorous stories with a unique twist on traditional fairytales. Each story can be compared to the original fairytale, or appreciated on its own. Fairytales are a key type of literary text found in the Common Core State Standards.

THE FOLLOWING BEFORE, DURING, AND AFTER READING ACTIVITY SUGGESTIONS SUPPORT LITERACY SKILL DEVELOPMENT AND CAN ENRICH SHARED READING EXPERIENCES:

1. Make reading fun! Choose a time to read when you and the child are relaxed and have time to share the story.

2. Before reading, invite the child to preview the book. The child can read the title, look at the illustrations, skim through the text, and make predictions as to what will happen in the story. Predicting sets a clear purpose for reading and learning.

3. During reading, encourage the child to monitor his or her understanding by asking questions to draw conclusions, making connections, and using context clues to understand unfamiliar words.

4. After reading, ask the child to review his or her predictions. Were they correct? Discuss different parts of the story, including main characters, setting, main events, and the problem and solution. If the child is familiar with the original fairytale, invite he or she to identify the similarities and differences between the two versions of the story.

5. Encourage the child to use his or her imagination to create fairytale jumbles based on other familiar stories.

6. Give praise! Children learn best in a positive environment.

IF YOU ENJOYED THIS BOOK, WHY NOT TRY ANOTHER TADPOLES: FAIRYTALE JUMBLES STORY?

VISIT WWW.CRABTREEBOOKS.COM FOR OTHER CRABTREE BOOKS.